Kalea Cavins

#2

MERCER MAYER'S
CRITTER KIDS® ADVENTURES

THE ALIEN
FROM OUTER SPACE
A GRAPHIC NOVEL ADVENTURE

D1122115

School Specialty
Publishing

Copyright © 2006 © 1995 Mercer Mayer Ltd.
Text for Page 32 © 2006 School Specialty Publishing.
Published by School Specialty Publishing, a member of the School Specialty Family.
A Big Tuna Trading Company, LLC/J. R. Sansevere Book
Originally published as The Alien.
Written by Erica Farber/J. R. Sansevere

ISBN 0-7696-4763-4

1 2 3 4 5 6 7 8 9 10 PHX 11 10 09 08 07 06

The Critter Kids were making a three-dimensional map of the solar system in school. They were looking forward to the weekend because a comet was supposed to pass through the atmosphere somewhere over Critterville.

COMETS are huge chunks of ice, rock, and dust orbiting the solar system. When they approach our sun, they heat up. That causes a tail of dust and gas to form behind them.

UNCLE ANDY IS COMING TO VISIT.

I'M GOING TO THE CRITTERVILLE MALL.

MY DAD AND I ARE GOING FISHING.

I'M GETTING MY HAIR CUT.

The SUN is actually a star that is 4.6 billion years old. More than a million Earths could fit inside it. The temperature at the sun's center is 27,000,000 degrees Fahrenheit.

When LC got home from school, there was a package for him from Uncle Andy. Inside was a powerful telescope. The card read: *I'll be watching the comet, too. Keep your eyes open—you never know what you may see!*

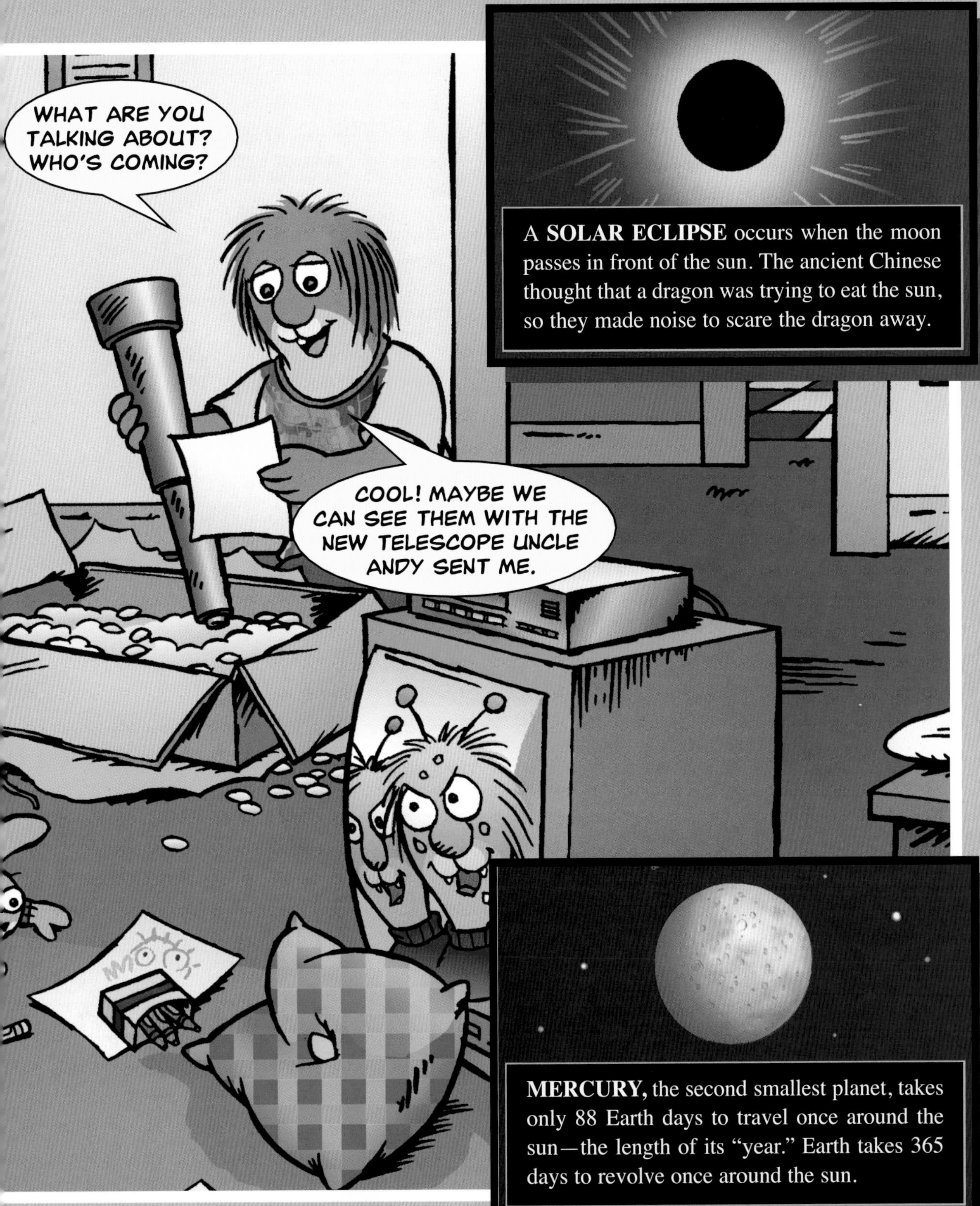
WHAT ARE YOU TALKING ABOUT? WHO'S COMING?
COOL! MAYBE WE CAN SEE THEM WITH THE NEW TELESCOPE UNCLE ANDY SENT ME.

A **SOLAR ECLIPSE** occurs when the moon passes in front of the sun. The ancient Chinese thought that a dragon was trying to eat the sun, so they made noise to scare the dragon away.

MERCURY, the second smallest planet, takes only 88 Earth days to travel once around the sun—the length of its "year." Earth takes 365 days to revolve once around the sun.

That night, LC invited all the Critter Kids over to camp out and look at the comet through his new telescope. While everyone sat around the campfire, LC began to tell them a story . . .

In the universe, there are many large groups of stars called *galaxies*. Earth is part of the **MILKY WAY GALAXY,** which contains billions of stars.

WELL, I NEVER TOLD ANYONE THIS BUT . . .

VENUS is the closest planet to Earth, but its surface temperature of 880 degrees Fahrenheit makes it too hot for us to visit. Its surface is drier than any desert on Earth.

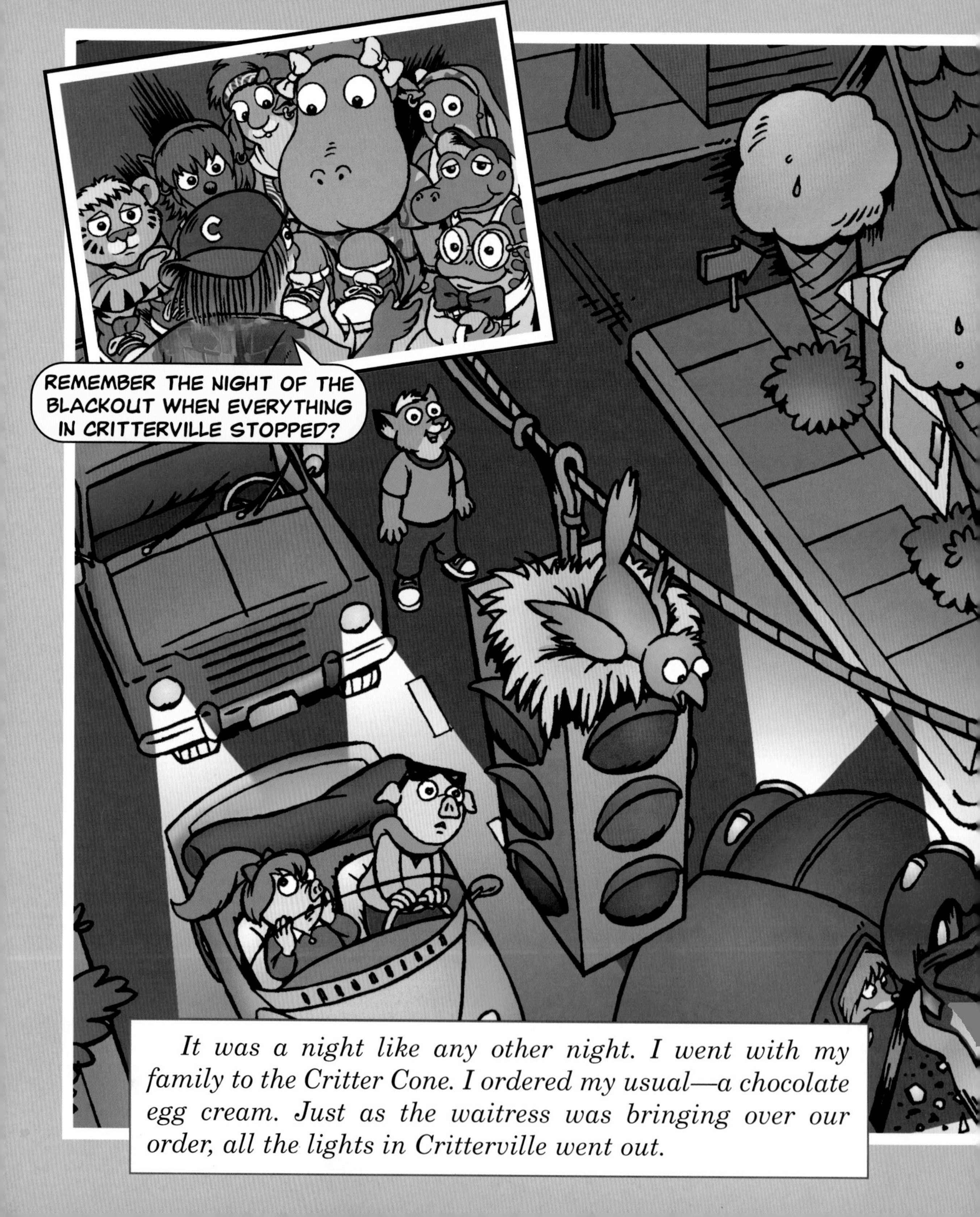
REMEMBER THE NIGHT OF THE BLACKOUT WHEN EVERYTHING IN CRITTERVILLE STOPPED?

It was a night like any other night. I went with my family to the Critter Cone. I ordered my usual—a chocolate egg cream. Just as the waitress was bringing over our order, all the lights in Critterville went out.

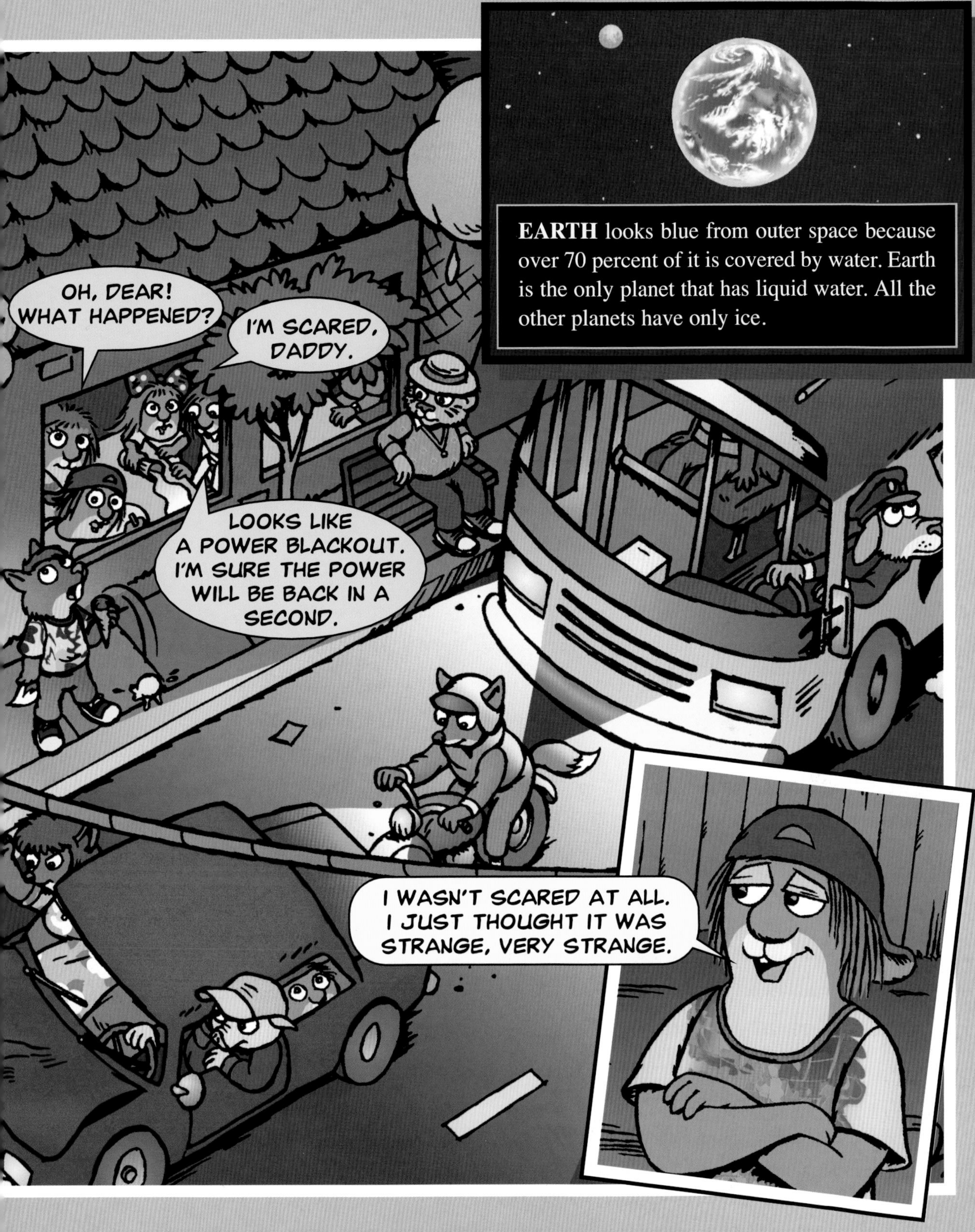
OH, DEAR! WHAT HAPPENED?
I'M SCARED, DADDY.
LOOKS LIKE A POWER BLACKOUT. I'M SURE THE POWER WILL BE BACK IN A SECOND.
I WASN'T SCARED AT ALL. I JUST THOUGHT IT WAS STRANGE, VERY STRANGE.

EARTH looks blue from outer space because over 70 percent of it is covered by water. Earth is the only planet that has liquid water. All the other planets have only ice.

I went to bed as usual, but I had a very weird feeling. Just as I was falling asleep, I heard a strange sound. It was a loud HUM-M-M. Then, the lights began to flash on and off. The bed started to shake, and all the toys in my room began to move by themselves. Outside my window, I saw these incredible flashing lights.

MARS is a red planet about half the size of Earth. Once, it probably flowed with water. Now, it is a windy desert world with canyons, craters, and mountains created by volcanoes.

I followed the strange lights into the woods. Then, I hid behind the Old Mill and watched as a giant flying saucer landed right by the lake.

JUPITER, the largest planet, is 11 times bigger than Earth. It would take about 6 months of nonstop travel to drive around it. To drive around Earth would take about 2 weeks.

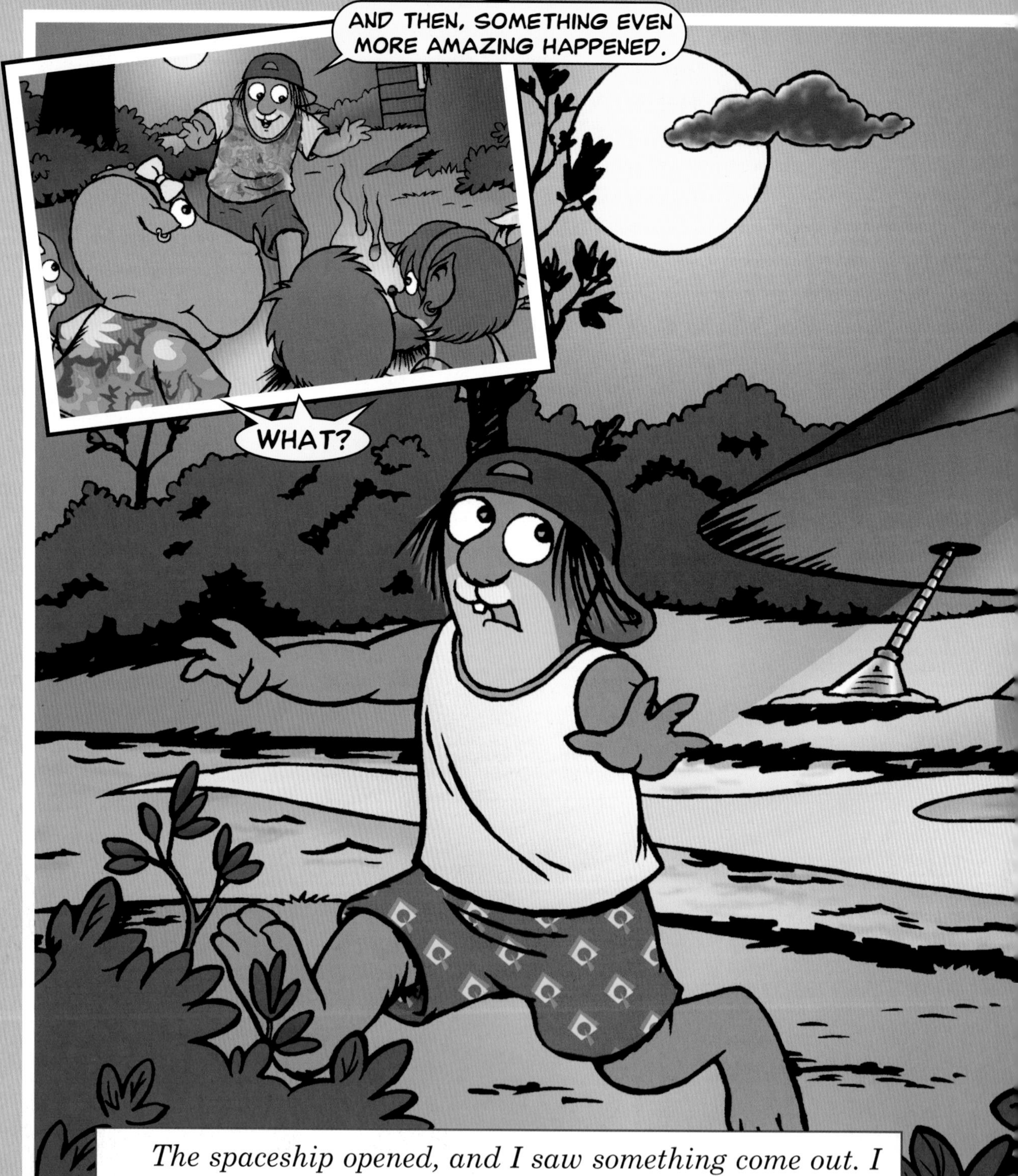
AND THEN, SOMETHING EVEN MORE AMAZING HAPPENED.
WHAT?

The spaceship opened, and I saw something come out. I turned around and ran as fast as I could. I never looked back.

SATURN is the second largest planet. Its has outer rings made of trillions of pieces of ice that never melt. The wind on Saturn sometimes blows at speeds over 1,000 miles per hour.

Calls came in from all over about the flying saucer. Later that night, the police surrounded it. Little did they know that an alien from the flying saucer was already loose somewhere in Critterville.

WE'VE GOT THE SPACECRAFT COMPLETELY SECURED. NOTHING CAN GET IN OR OUT.

URANUS has 42 years of sunlight, followed by 42 years of darkness. Orbiting it are 11 dark rings that are so thin, the first ones weren't even discovered until 1977.

The alien was out there somewhere. It was up to Yo Yo and me to find him. We went outside. I saw a strange light glowing inside the clubhouse. I just knew the alien was in there.

NEPTUNE takes almost 165 years to orbit the sun. It has a huge dark spot the size of Earth known as the *Great Dark Spot*, which is a stormy weather system in its atmosphere.

I couldn't believe it! There was the alien playing my favorite video game. He was an awesome player! We played all night long.

PLUTO is the smallest planet and is also the farthest from the sun. Because it is made mostly of ice, it is very cold. Pluto's temperature is more than 350 degrees below zero Fahrenheit.

In the morning, we were both really hungry. We went inside to get some breakfast. I sat at the table, and the alien crawled underneath. My dad made a whole lot of pancakes. The alien ate almost every single one.

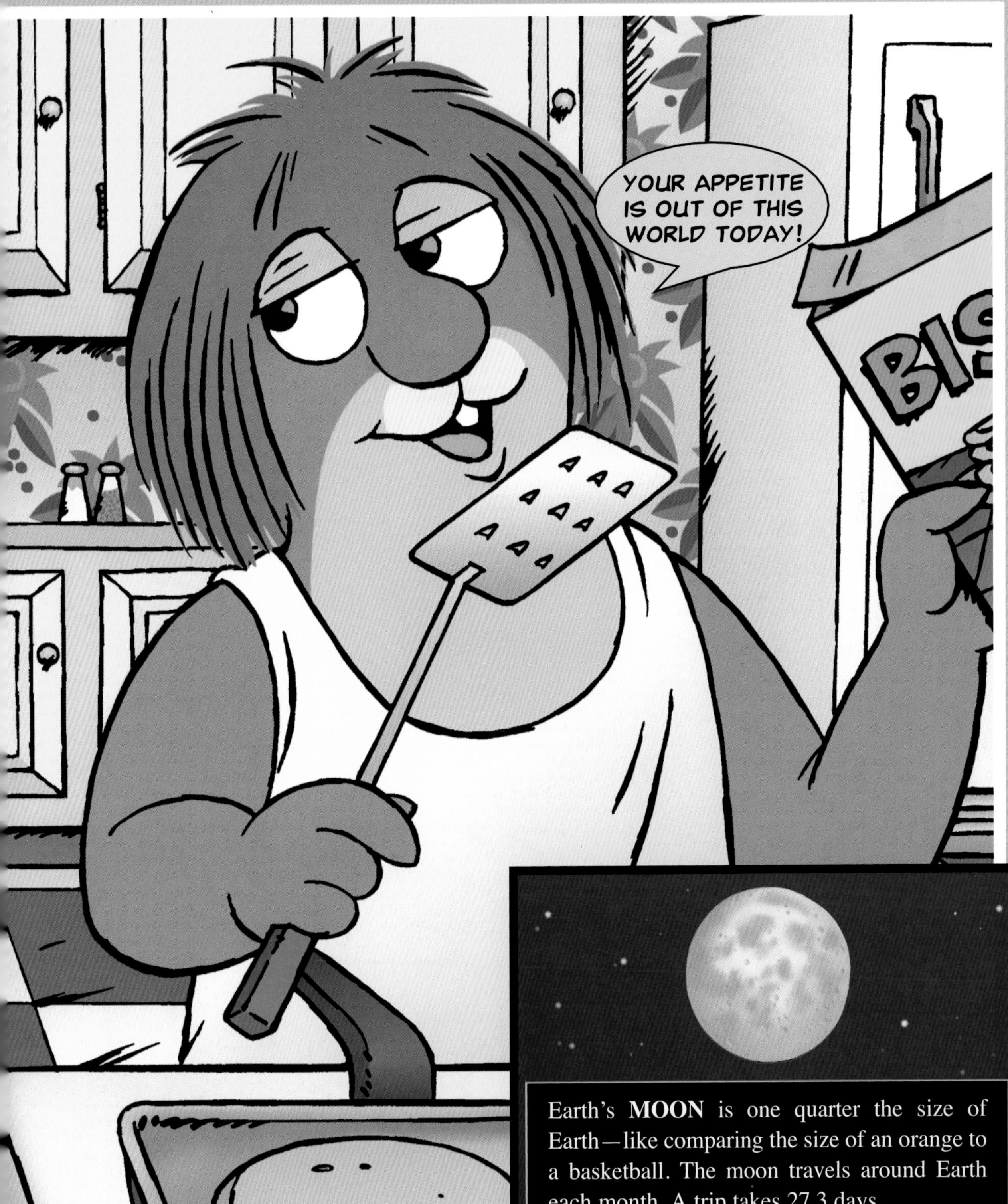
YOUR APPETITE IS OUT OF THIS WORLD TODAY!

Earth's **MOON** is one quarter the size of Earth—like comparing the size of an orange to a basketball. The moon travels around Earth each month. A trip takes 27.3 days.

After breakfast, the alien took the chip from inside my video game to fix his spaceship. Now all he had to do was get back to his spaceship without getting caught.

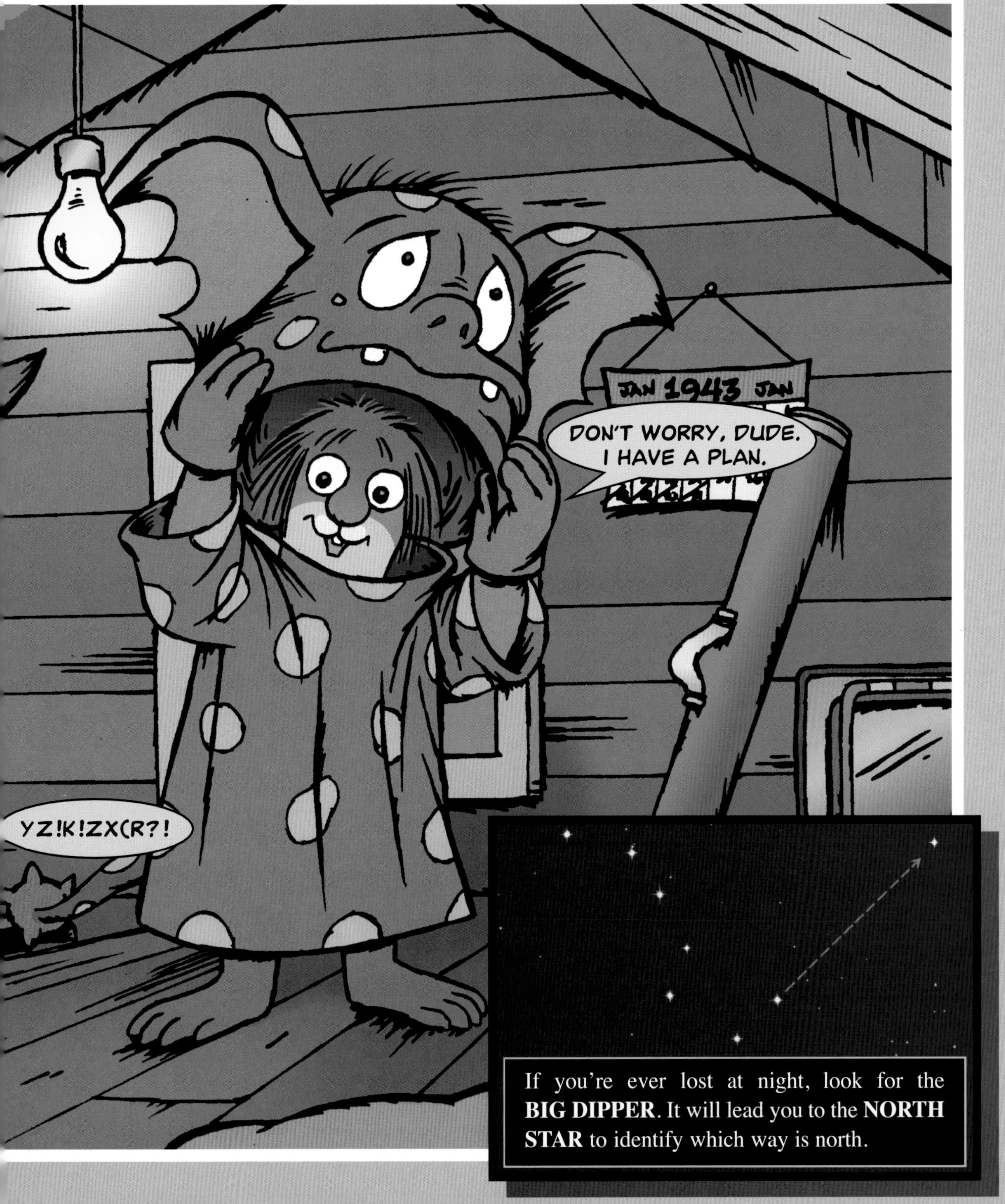
JAN 1943 JAN
DON'T WORRY, DUDE. I HAVE A PLAN.
YZ!K!ZX(R?!

If you're ever lost at night, look for the **BIG DIPPER**. It will lead you to the **NORTH STAR** to identify which way is north.

My plan worked perfectly. Everyone thought I was the alien. Meanwhile, the real alien was on his way back to his spaceship.

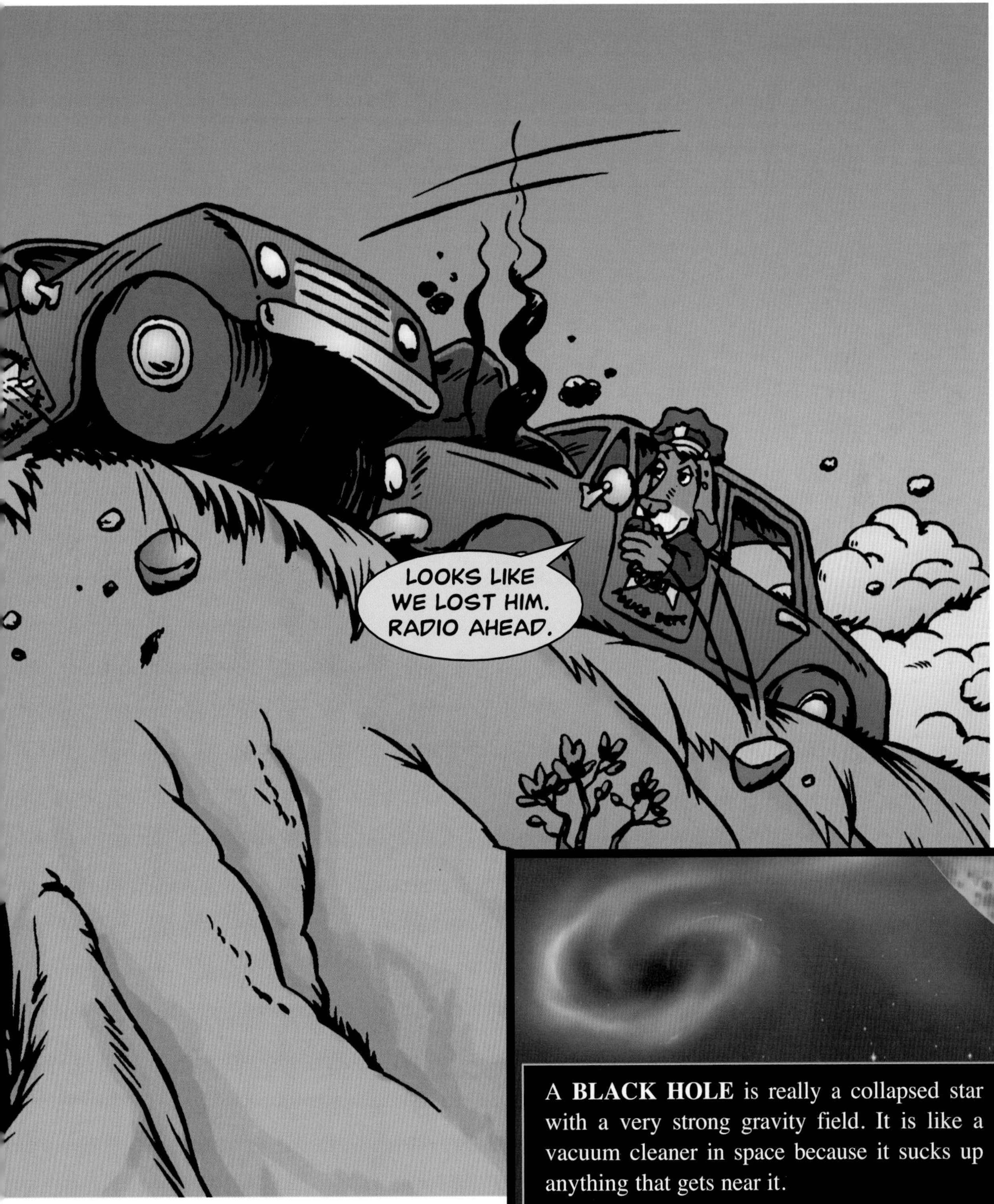
LOOKS LIKE
WE LOST HIM.
RADIO AHEAD.

A **BLACK HOLE** is really a collapsed star with a very strong gravity field. It is like a vacuum cleaner in space because it sucks up anything that gets near it.

The police finally caught up with me. They had me surrounded. They still thought I was the alien, so I took off my costume. Just then, the spaceship flew overhead and the alien waved good-bye.

SHOOTING STARS are really meteors—pieces of debris from space that turn into streaks of light as they burn up and pass into our atmosphere.

OH, I FORGOT TO TELL YOU. THE ALIEN SAID HE WANTED TO COME BACK TO MEET MY FRIENDS.

After LC finished telling his story, the Critter Kids went into the tent to go to sleep. Suddenly, the tent began to shake and there was a weird glowing light outside. Everyone started screaming. LC just smiled.

Some scientists believe that there is a tenth planet beyond Pluto that has not yet been discovered. They call it **PLANET X**.

Vocabulary

atmosphere—the whole mass of air surrounding a planet. *Shortly before landing, the space shuttle entered Earth's atmosphere.*

canyons—deep narrow valleys with steep sides that often have a stream of water flowing through them. *Looking at rivers at the bottom of canyons sometimes makes me dizzy.*

crater—a depression formed by the impact of a meteorite. *Using powerful telescopes, astronomers are able to see the craters on the moon.*

Fahrenheit—a measurement of temperature. *The average temperature of your body is 98.6 degrees Fahrenheit.*

orbiting—traveling in a circular pattern around an object. *Earth is constantly orbiting around the sun.*

revolve—to go around in a circle. *It takes Earth a year—or 365 days—to revolve around the sun.*

solar system—the sun and everything that revolves around it because of its gravitational pull. *The Critter Kids used a telescope to learn about the planets in our solar system.*

The Story and You

What does LC suggest was the cause of the power blackout?

Do you think LC's story really happened? What makes you choose your answer?

How is a telescope similar to binoculars? How are they different?

If you discovered a new planet in our solar system, what would you name it? Why?